To the friends who have helped me through dark times.

Boy Seeking Band is published by Capstone Young Readers,
1710 Roe Crest Drive, North Mankato, Minnesota 56003
www.mycapstone.com

Cataloging-in-Publication Data is available on the Library of Congress website.
ISBN 978-1-4965-4449-0 (library hardcover)
ISBN 978-1-4965-4453-7 (eBook)

Summary: After transferring from a private arts school to a public school,
prodigy bass player Terence Kato quickly puts together a band, but winning
a citywide music competition with a brand-new drummer won't be as easy as
"ONE...TWO...THREE...FOUR!"

Cover illustration and design by Brann Garvey

Printed in the United States of America.
010368F17

DRUMMER WANTED

BY STEVE BREZENOFF

STONE ARCH BOOKS
a capstone imprint

TABLE OF CONTENTS

INTRODUCTION

Terence Kato is a prodigy bass player, but he's determined to finish middle school on a high note. Life has other plans. In the middle of eighth grade, he's forced to transfer from a private arts school to a public school, where the kids seemingly speak a different language. But he knows a universal one: music.

He quickly puts together a band, but winning a citywide music competition with a brand-new drummer won't be as easy as "ONE...TWO... THREE...FOUR!"

CHAPTER ONE

It's Saturday afternoon and early March in Minneapolis. Outside, the air is crisp and dry, the sky as clear blue and beautiful as any perfect summer day, but the trees are bare, and the lawns are covered in layered blankets of snow.

Mounds of frozen slush stained gray by car exhaust, street salt, and sand line the sidewalks and trap the odd car and bicycle whose owner didn't move them in time for the plows.

But in the basement of the Viateur home — where the slim windows set high in the walls have been covered by soundproof foam and thick black curtains — you'd never know it. It's warm and dim, lit only by a pair of lamps in opposite corners and a string of Christmas lights that run along the crown molding.

The four members of the still unnamed new band gathered twenty minutes ago, and have already played through three songs from bandleader and bassist Terence Kato's set.

"They sound really good," he says as he clicks on his bass's tuning pedal and checks the open A string.

"Yeah," says Meredith "Eddie" Carson, the band's singer and the first person Terence met at Franklin Middle School, where all of the bandmembers are students. "I'm so glad we got a drummer!"

Well, all the bandmembers except one: James, the drummer. He's sixteen, a waiter at Paulie's Pizza, and perpetually late.

"It would be nice if James were on time,"

says Novia, the harp virtuoso, as he plucks a syncopated line that bounces between the bass and treble strings of her instrument. "I mean, now and then."

The pianist, Claude, whose basement they're in, plays a high trill. "If he brings pizza to every practice, he can be late to every practice."

As if on cue, the doorbell rings upstairs and they hear Ms. Viateur's hurried footsteps across the first floor. A moment later, James is hurrying down the basement steps, his heavy-duty laptop case under one arm and a pizza in his hands.

"Check this out," he says, and he drops the pizza in the center of the basement floor and tosses his laptop onto the couch next to the half-reclined Eddie.

"Pineapple?" Eddie asks, bored-sounding and bored-looking.

"What?" James says as he pulls a folded paper from his back pocket. "Oh, the pizza. No.

Peppers. Messed-up order so they let me take it. It's probably cold. But look at this."

He unfolds the paper and drops it on top of the pizza box. Claude, who was already up to get a slice of pizza, kneels beside the box. Eddie leans off the couch a little. Terence keeps his bass around his neck and shoulders and leans between them. He recognizes the logo at the top of the flyer at once.

"What is it?" Novia says.

Terence reads aloud: "The Wellstone Music Battle of the KID Bands. May fourteenth. All band members must be sixteen or younger."

"That's us," Novia says.

Terence nods as Eddie picks up the paper and leans back on the couch with it. Claude opens the pizza box and take a slice.

"First place prize is a gift certificate for ten *thousand* dollars," Eddie says, reading from the paper, "and recording time, *and* a slot on a store-sponsored and -produced compilation."

"Wow," Terence says.

"That's only two thousand for each of us," Novia points out.

"Only?" Eddie says. "I'll take it."

Terence nods again. "Think we can be ready in time?" he says. "It's only two months away. I'd been meaning to mention it, but I wasn't sure everyone would be into the idea."

"Very into it," Claude says with a full mouth.

"Man, I'm ready *now*," Eddie says as she folds the paper into an airplane.

"I don't know," Terence says. "I remember this battle from last year. My band didn't even enter — since my mom was sick. But I heard the competition was tough."

"Absolutely," James says, sitting down and opening his laptop. "I've gone to the last three battles. Bands come from all over the state. It's no joke. And you know who won last year."

Claude shakes his head.

Terence says it solemnly: "Time Stereo."

"Yup," James says. "Look at them now."

"Come on," Eddie says as James pulls his cables across her lap to reach the PA. "You're telling me Time Stereo are only big today because they won some dumb battle of the bands? Please."

"Why not?" Novia says.

"Because their YouTube channel has like three million subscribers?" Eddie says. "They didn't get all of them from a battle of the bands sponsored by a Podunk music store."

"Maybe," James says, "but it's a good enough endorsement for me."

"Me too," Claude says, taking a second slice.

Eddie tosses her paper airplane across the room so it hits Terence in the face.

"Hey!" he says.

"You know what we need, though," she says, "if we're going to sign up for this battle?"

"Five bucks each for the entry fee," James says.

Eddie kicks him. "I mean," she says, "what we need is a name."

"And quick," James says. "Entrance deadline is next Friday."

"OK," Terence says. "So we have a few days to think about it. Anyone have any ideas?"

No one says anything.

Terence sighs. "And I guess we'll need a few days."

CHAPTER TWO

On Monday morning, Terence climbs off his
bus with Eddie. They've ridden the bus together
since Terence changed schools in January, only
missing a morning here and there, right after
she found out his mom had died.

This morning, they part in the front hall with
a fist bump. Eddie slips in earbuds and says,
"Hot new tracks."

Terence knows she's listening to their band
— the "demo" songs James recorded. They're
not exactly professional recordings, but despite

being the most obnoxious server at Paulie's, the guy knows a thing or two about production.

At his audition, he recorded two of the songs they played together. On Saturday — after deciding to enter the battle of the bands — he recorded four more songs and emailed them to his middle school bandmates.

"They're rough, OK?" Terence says, holding on to Eddie's hand before she hurries off to her advisory class. "Don't play them for anyone."

"I know, I know," she says, pulling her hand away. "Don't worry about it, OK?"

"Don't worry so much!" she says, and then she waves as she walks fast down the front hall to her locker.

"They sound *good*," Novia says. She sits next to Terence in advisory.

"I know," Terence says. He's excited about the demo tracks, but he wants them to be perfect. "Did you play them for anyone?"

She shakes her head. "Just my sister and brother this morning," she says. Her sister is in elementary school and her brother is a high school senior. "Rosa danced all over the living room. Santino said it was garbage and turned off the speakers on Mom and Dad's computer."

"How nice." Terence scratches his pen across the back of his spiral notebook, absentmindedly trying to come up with band names. He hasn't had a single idea yet.

Novia shrugs. "Sonny's a moron. He doesn't like anything I like. His opinion is invalid."

"And Rosa?" Terence asks.

"She's nine," Novia admits with a shrug. "If it's music, she dances to it."

The bell rings to end advisory, and they have a few minutes before first hour. Most of them stay in the same room, though, so no one gets up. They just start talking slightly louder.

One of the few kids whose advisory is in a different classroom shows up and drops into the desk in front of Novia. "No," she says — a nickname, not a negative, "those songs you sent me this morning are so good."

"Thanks," Novia says, glancing at Terence as her face goes red. "I guess I sent it to Gina too. Do you know Gina?"

"No," Terence says. "Nice to meet you."

"You too," she says. "Have you heard it?"

"Um, yes," Terence says.

"Terence is in the band with me!" Novia says.

Gina doesn't seem especially impressed by that, and the buzzer rings to start first hour. Gina hurries to her spot near the front.

"So you didn't just play it for your sister and brother," Terence says quietly.

"Yes, I did!" Novia insists quietly. "I didn't play it for Gina. I just *sent* it to her. She's been my best friend since like kindergarten, Terence."

"Did you *send* it to anyone else?"

"I'm sorry," she whispers. "I'm proud of it, you know?"

How can Terence be mad? He's proud of it too, even if the production isn't ideal. "Yeah, I know," he says. "Don't worry about it. Maybe everyone will like it."

At lunch, Terence finds Eddie at their usual spot. Unusually, though, she isn't alone. Even more unusually, the people surrounding her chair at their table are not Luke and Claude, or even Novia, or one of Eddie's pre-band friends he sees around sometimes.

These are strangers. He recognizes two of them from his own class schedule, but the rest are only vaguely familiar from the halls. A few seem to be in seventh or even sixth grade.

Whoever they are, they seem to adore Eddie.

"Um, hi," Terence says as he walks up to the gaggle of admirers surrounding his singer.

Eddie looks up and jumps to her feet, almost knocking her chair over. "Terry!" she says, and quickly, "I mean Terence. Isn't this *amazing*?"

"What is *this*, exactly?" Terence says, dropping his bag on the chair next to Eddie.

"They all love our band!" Eddie says.

Terence opens his mouth but nothing comes out. He only stares at the gang of onlookers.

"Come on," Eddie says, grabbing Terence by the elbow and pulling him to the snack-bar line. Their "new fans" stay behind, talking among themselves, presumably about how amazing Eddie is. "Can you believe it?"

Terence, practically gaping at the crowd back at their table as he steps into the snack bar, says, "Not really."

Just then, Novia sprints into the snack bar with them. "You guys!" she squeals.

"Right?" Eddie says, and the two girls throw their arms around each other in celebration.

"How many people did you send the songs to?" Terence says, trying to get their attention.

Eddie shrugs and holds Novia in a half embrace. "Maybe ten?"

"Easily ten," Novia says. "And Gina sent it to a few people, she says. I don't know."

"Don't look some glum," Eddie says, poking Terence in the belly. "Everyone likes it! This is *amazing* news."

"I don't know . . . ," Terence says.

"What's not to know?" Novia says. "Do you know how many compliments I got just walking to the cafeteria from my last class?"

Terence would like to explain — how he counted on being invisible at this school, how he didn't want to make waves or even ripples, how he hoped to escape into the sea of the huge high school in the fall as anonymous as possible.

These two would never understand.

"I'm buying you a bagel, T-man!" Eddie says as she bounds to the counter to order.

"T-man?" he mutters, Novia laughing beside him. His phone vibrates in his pocket at the same moment Novia's chirps a harp solo of Bach's "Jesu, Joy of Man's Desiring," and Eddie's belts out the opening pogo sound of Bikini Kill's "Rebel Girl."

Terence pulls out his phone as the girls do the same. "It's from James," he says, and reads to himself: *Um guys what DID YOU DO???*

"Uh-oh," Novia says, her eyes going wide.

"What?" Terence says as Eddie huddles up with them. "What is he talking about?"

Novia shakes her head. "It can't be," she whispers, and at the same moment Claude comes into the snack bar.

"Yo," he says, strutting up to the counter. He orders a chicken griller with fruit salad, and then says over his shoulder to his bandmates. "Get that text from James?"

They all nod.

"According to Scotty's big sister," Claude says, "who is in eleventh, our demo is being played over the school-wide PA at East High."

Terence's phone slips from his hand and drops to the floor. So much for anonymity.

"I don't see what the big deal is," Claude says, taking a huge bite of his chicken sandwich.

Their fans have dispersed, leaving the band members to enjoy their lunches in peace.

Inside, though, Terence isn't peaceful.

"How?" he says. "How could this happen?"

"It's Sonny," Novia says. "It has to be."

"Why?" Terence says.

"Well," Novia drawls, pushing the last piece of fruit, "he said he hated it. So either he lied and wanted to spread it all over the high school, or he really thought it was terrible and wanted to embarrass us."

Claude taps his nose.

Novia sticks her tongue out at him. "Anyway," she says, "his girlfriend works in the main office one hour every day."

"And she uses the PA system?" Terence says.

"She does the announcements," Novia says, shrugging. "I think."

"You know," Eddie breaks in, "that's not a bad name for a band."

"What? The Announcements?" Terence asks.

"No." Eddie laughs. "Public Address System."

"I don't hate it," says Claude.

"Me either," Novia agrees.

"Could be a little — I don't know — *jazzier?*" says Terence, unimpressed.

"What about PA System?" Eddie offers. "Maybe PA Quintet."

"Maybe," Terence echoes.

"That means yes," says Eddie with a smile.

Just then, all their phones chime again. Only Claude doesn't flinch. He just takes another huge bite of his chicken sandwich.

So. Everyone loves it. But Lucy's in trouble.

"That's Sonny's girlfriend," Novia says.

"I thought her name was Sandra," Claude says, furrowing his brow.

"They broke up after Christmas," Novia says.

"Huh."

"Um, guys?" Eddie says, her grin lit up like a string of lights. "Who cares about Santino's love life? Everyone loves our band. We've got the battle of the bands in the bag."

"Remember what James said," Terence says, "There'll be bands from all over the state. There might be bands from Hart Arts too."

"Ooh," Novia says. "I'm *so* scared."

Eddie and Claude laugh.

"Fine, laugh," Terence says. "But I promise there will be serious competition."

"Stop worrying, worrier," Eddie says as she stands up to bus her tray.

Terence crosses his arms. "I can't help it."

"No kidding," Claude says, elbowing him lightly and then stealing a chunk of his bagel.

Terence grunts. "I'm not hungry anyway."

The newly named PA Quintet keeps up rehearsals of course, twice during the week and then again on Saturday afternoon.

James manages to make it almost on time.

"No pizza, though," Claude points out.

The Saturday afternoon is a full run-through of all the songs they've been learning together. They're still mostly tunes Terence performed with the Kato Quintet back at Hart, but a few wouldn't work with this lineup. Of course, thanks to Novia's and Eddie's influence on the sound, he added a few songs too.

"Feeling any better?" Eddie says as the band packs up.

Terence has begun leaving his bass in the Viateurs' house, so today — with mid-March offering up the first spring-like day in months — he biked to practice.

"Yeah, I guess," he says. "We sound good. Should be ready for the battle in seven weeks."

"That's the spirit," James says when he's halfway up the stairs, his laptop dangling from one hand. "See you dorks next week."

Novia zips up her harp's bag and Claude

rises from the piano to help her bring it up the basement steps. She can't leave it here because she still sees her private harp teacher twice a week at her house.

"You leaving too?" Terence says.

Eddie shakes her head and drops onto the old, ratty couch. "My mom won't be here for another twenty minutes." She pulls the Viateur's old acoustic guitar out from under the couch and waggles her eyebrows. "I'll amuse myself."

"OK," Terence says. "Good job today."

"Thanks, boss," she says, saluting.

Terence rolls his eyes and heads upstairs. At his bike, he realizes he left his phone in the basement. "Dang it."

Novia's car skids away from the curb and Claude goes back inside. Terence jogs to follow him and rings the bell.

"Forget something?" asks Ms. Viateur.

"Phone," Terence says.

Claude's mom steps aside.

Terence hurries to the basement steps and freezes at the top. He expected to find Eddie and Claude, joking or even playing music together, but Claude is in the kitchen pouring himself a bowl of cereal. From the top of the basement steps, though, he can hear Eddie.

She's playing one of her own again, and her guitar playing is a bit better this time. Her voice is too. Maybe that's his imagination. He's been hanging out with her a lot, after all, and has gotten to like her. As a friend.

Terence stands there, listening to her voice and her words and the melody she's written.

"What are you doing?"" Claude says, coming up behind him, his mouth full of something crunchy and smelling of sugar.

"Nothing!" Terence says. "Forgot my phone."

"OK," Claude says, heading back to the kitchen. "Go get it then."

Downstairs, Eddie stops playing. Terence hurries into the basement.

"Hello," Eddie says, the guitar on her lap.

"Forgot my phone," Terence says.

"I know," Eddie says. "It's right there." She nods toward the arm of the couch.

"Thanks," Terence says, scooping it up. "Well, bye again."

He bikes home pedaling furiously, his heart pounding maybe not just from the exertion.

On Sunday morning, Dad is up and dressed and sipping coffee at the kitchen table, scrolling through his phone, when Terence comes in, still groggy with sleep.

"Kiddo," Dad says. "Gotta hit the mall."

"What?" Terence says, dropping into the seat across from Dad. "Why?"

Terence can't remember the last time his dad went to the mall, never mind willingly.

"I need work clothes," Dad says.

"You work at home," Terence says, and adds in his mind, *Or you used to.*

Dad's freelance graphic design and illustration work has been pretty sparse the last few months. Terence hoped as Dad worked through his depression, he'd start working more again. Maybe this is a good sign.

"Well," Dad says, picking up his phone again and setting it right down, "I have a job interview on Tuesday morning."

"Seriously?" Terence says. "For an office job?"

"Is that so far-fetched?" Dad says, as if he's offended.

"It's been a while," Terence says.

"Eight years," Dad says. "Not so long."

"I don't know, Dad," Terence says. "A lot's changed. Have you heard of the 'Internet'?"

"You're hilarious," Dad says and takes a long drink of his coffee. "Now get dressed. I want to be there before it gets crowded."

Terence splits off from his dad at the first discount-designer clothing store and heads to the southeast corner of the mall — the weird part. It's where the dollar store is and the place that only sells items made of alpaca fur, and Keys, Strings, Skins, and More, the only musical instrument store in the mall. It doesn't get a lot of traffic, but they still let anyone who comes by play the electric piano near the entrance.

Terence used to spend a lot of time here when his mom and dad took him to the mall when he was little. He even got to know the manager, Hillary. Today, though, is Sunday, and Hillary isn't working.

Terence sits on the bench at the electric piano, switches it to church organ, and plays the opening of "Whiter Shade of Pale."

"Ooh, haven't heard anyone play *that* before," says a very familiar and snarky voice.

Terence looks up from the keys, and there's Polly Winger.

Terence's fingers slip from the keys into his lap.

"Hi, Terence." She opens her arms for a hug.

"Polly," Terence says, clumsily standing up and putting one arm around her. "Hi."

"I haven't talked to you in so long," Polly says. "How are you doing?" She asks in that particular way — with sadness in her voice and that crease between her eyebrows — so he knows what she means. *Are you still sad that your mom died?*

As if he'll ever stop.

"I'm OK," he says with a shrug. "Um, how's everyone at Hart?"

"You know, same as always." Polly rolls her eyes. "Of course we had to change the name of the quintet and bring in Noel from ninth to play bass for you."

"Oh," Terence says, looking at his feet. "Yeah, I started a new band, actually."

Polly's eyes go wide. "Wow, really?" she says. "I didn't know they even had a music program at Franklin."

"Yeah, well," Terence says, "it's not very good. But there are a handful of talented kids."

"Bet your singer isn't as good as me, though, huh," Polly says, tossing a joking elbow at him.

Terence feels his face go hot.

"Aw, don't worry," Polly says, letting him off the hook. "I'm sure the new singer is wonderful too. Is it another jazz combo?"

Terence opens his mouth to answer and remembers the phone in his pocket. He grins as he pulls it out and clicks open the tracks James recorded. "Sort of," he says. "Listen."

Polly looks doubtful as she takes his phone and puts the speaker to her ear. "She *is* good," she says when Eddie's vocals come in. "Tone's a bit thin."

"You're listening to her on a phone," Terence says. "Once you hear it with headph—"

"Is that . . . ," Polly says, cutting him off. "Is that *electronic drums?*"

"Yeah," Terence says. "Sounds good, right?"

She shrugs. Before the song is over, she hands him the phone back. "It sounds pretty good."

"Just *pretty* good?" Terence says, getting a little irritated with Polly's Hart Arts snobbery. He goes on before he can stop himself. "Everyone at Franklin loves it."

Polly grins wickedly. "Mmhm," she says. "A student body who thinks jazz is a basketball team and classical music begins and ends with Pachelbel's Canon in D."

Terence is fuming. He shoves his phone into his pocket, prepared to storm off, but instead he opens his big mouth one more time. "Yeah, well we'll be playing the battle of the bands in May. We'll see what the judges think."

Polly's grin vanishes. "*You're* entering?" she says. "*We're* entering. Terence, we used to be friends. You're competing against us now?"

"Key words being 'used to,'" Terence spits.

"Ha!" Polly says. "Like you've been Mister In-Touch since you left."

"Whatever," Terence says. *At least I have an excuse.*

"Yeah, whatever to you," Polly says. "See at the battle, public-school boy."

With that, she flips her hair and walks away. Terence watches her till she sits with a group of her friends who'd been watching the whole thing from the coffee shop at the far end of the corridor.

"Thought I'd find you here," says Dad as he walks up behind him. "Was that Polly Winger?"

"Yeah," Terence says, still staring at his former friend. "Are you done shopping?"

"Yup," Dad says. "Wanna get some lunch in the food court? Something fast and fried and greasy?"

"I'm not hungry," Terence says, and without waiting for Dad, walks fast toward the parking ramp.

CHAPTER THREE

As Minneapolis thaws completely, the PA Quintet meets more and more often. Hockey season ends, so Claude is available for practice practically every day. Novia still has her harp lesson, and James still has to work the dinner shift at Paulie's now and then, but even then the rest of the band often gets together to run through their set list minus one.

It's dinnertime one Saturday at the beginning of May, and the PA Quintet has been practicing most of the day. Now they lounge around in the Viateurs' media room. Ms. V loaded up two trays of pizza rolls, set out cut veggies and ranch dip, and stocked the mini-fridge with every drink she imagined the band would like.

Terence sits on the floor with his legs under the coffee table and his back against Eddie's legs, who lounges in the cushy gaming chair.

"I'm telling you," James says. "We have the battle on lock. We sound sick."

"Sick," Novia says, nodding, just before she chomps a celery stick.

Terence laughs and pops a pizza roll in his mouth — and immediately regrets it. The molten core explodes in his mouth, leaving him gasping. He reaches for his juice pouch. Empty.

Eddie shoves her own pouch into his hand.

Terence takes a long pull — it's peach flavor and he hates peach, but it doesn't matter. It's nearly empty when he puts it down on the coffee table. "Thanks," he says, breathless.

"You," Claude says, grabbing a handful of pizza rolls, "are an amateur." He pops the pizza rolls into his mouth and chews slowly with his mouth open, gasping in breaths of cool air.

"See," he says, "you don't let them burst. You make them leak slowly."

"Sounds delicious," Eddie says.

"Oh, it is," Claude says, wiping his mouth with the back of his hand. "It is."

"Claude!" his mom snaps as she happens past the doorway. "Napkin!"

"Sorry, Mom!" Claude says, grabbing a paper napkin from the stack next to the veggies plate. "I swear, she has a sixth sense."

Everyone laughs. It's hard to be sure whether they're laughing with Claude or at him, but he doesn't seem to care either way. Lounging there on the floor with Eddie cracking up behind him, Novia across from him, and Claude and James on the couch, Terence feels a warmth that he hasn't felt in a long time.

He knows what it is, of course, but maybe if he doesn't say it — if no one says anything about it — having a new group of friends won't be so bad.

Terence is sitting there, his mind wandering like that, a smile on his face, when Eddie squeezes his shoulder and says something.

"Hm?" he says, looking up at her and finding her upside-down face looking back. She's not laughing now, though. She's not even smiling.

"Oh," Claude says from the couch, and he's not laughing anymore either.

What happened? Terence wonders.

"I'm sorry," Claude says, leaning forward, his elbows on his knees. "I didn't know."

"Me either," James says. "Man, that sucks."

Terence looks across the table at Novia, whose eyes are full with tears. She doesn't say anything, but it's obvious what's happened.

Terence stands up. "See?" he snaps, turning to face Eddie. "See what happens?"

"What?" Eddie says, reaching for him. "What do —"

Terence dodges, almost tripping over the coffee table, sending the platter of pizza rolls across the floor. The little puffs of orange pastry scatter like mice: under furniture, into corners, out of sight.

"No," Terence says. "This is why I didn't want friends, don't you get it? Don't you see what happens? It's contagious. It's like a *stink* I can't wash off, and now all of them know about it. They all can smell it now."

Eddie stands. "Terence, I —"

"No!" he snaps again, backing away. "I'm leaving now. No more friends. No more hanging out. No more band. It's over. Goodbye."

Terence turns his back on the Public Address Quintet, walks out of the Viateurs' house, slams the door behind him, and bikes home fast enough so the wind dries the tears on his face.

CHAPTER FOUR

The first two weeks of May should have been good ones. Dad got that job, and he started the following Monday. He's getting up every morning as early as Terence. He's shaving and dressing and focusing on work. He's coming home tired but energized, smiling some days and with stories over dinner about the new job.

In fact, Dad is acting a little like Terence probably was when he was meeting new people he liked and enjoying band rehearsal.

So the first two weeks of May *should* have been and *could* have been good ones. But instead Terence spends them mostly alone. He ignores loads of texts from the former PA Quintet.

From James, to the group: *So we can just assume T's meltdown is forgiven and everything's cool and practice Tuesday afternoon right?*

From Claude, to the group: *T we all promise never to mention it again and you don't smell.*

From Novia, to Terence: *I'm sorry Terence. Please come out of hiding,* which is almost amusing because she was sitting right next to him in advisory when she sent that one.

And from Eddie, to Terence and to the group, dozens of texts, apologizing to him, scolding him, lecturing him on friendship.

Terence deletes them from his phone and refuses to make eye contact in the halls. At lunch, he hides out in the media center.

But even though they only met several months ago, Eddie knows Terence well enough.

It's Friday lunchtime on May 13, and Terence is at the last table in the media center with his head down when someone sits across from him.

Terence doesn't look up. People share the big tables in the media center all the time. It could be anyone.

Of course it's not. Out of the corner of his eye he sees the ragged cuffs of a red plaid shirt and dark hands folded together. On one hand is a gold ring with a green gem, the kind you can buy for fifty cents from one of those machines in front of the grocery store. Eddie.

"Terence," she whispers, and her voice is not mad, not exactly. But it has the tone of someone who's about ready to give up on him. "I can't understand what you've been going through."

Terence doesn't look up. He clenches his jaw, wishing she'd stop talking, but also not wanting her to leave.

"If I lost my mom . . . ," she says. "I don't even know what I'd do. I'm sure I'd lash out. A lot. I'd probably flip over this table and punch someone in the face."

Terence thinks about himself flipping the table and almost laughs as his eyes fill with tears.

"But I know that I'm your friend," she says. "And Claude is, and Novia." After a beat, she adds, "I don't know about James."

Terence laughs and covers it with a sniff.

"And I know that your life *will* continue," she goes on, "whether you choose to live it or not."

Terence still says nothing. Tears drop from his eyes onto the hand he's using as a pillow.

"Your friends would like to live it with you," she says, "with or without the band."

After a few moments, she pushes back her chair and stands up. Terence lifts his head and watches her leave the media center.

"Was that Eddie Carson?" says a sixth-grade boy, walking up to his table, his awe-filled eyes on the closing media center doors.

Terence nods.

"Isn't she amazing?" the boy says. "Her band is my favorite ever." He's practically swooning as he walks off.

That evening, Terence is sitting at the kitchen table doing his homework — or trying to — when Dad gets home from work.

"Hey, kiddo," Dad says. He grabs a soda from the fridge and sits across from him. "How's the homework going?"

Terence shakes his head. "It's not."

"Need some help?" Dad says, craning his neck to get a look at the upside-down notebook and textbook. "Ooh, polynomial equations. Might be beyond my abilities."

"I just can't focus," Terence says.

"Something on your mind?" Dad says.

It's been a long time since Terence spoke to his dad about anything like this. In fact, even years ago, when something was bothering Terence — something at school going wrong, or some kids making fun of him — he usually went to Mom for comfort, support, or advice.

But that's not an option, so Terence takes a deep breath and lays it all out, nearly everything that's happened to him since he started at Franklin Middle School: meeting Eddie, starting the band, tomorrow's competition.

Dad knows some of it, but the details — and Terence's explosion two weeks ago — Terence hasn't shared until now.

"This is going to sound a little weird right now," Dad says, "but I'm very proud of you."

"Why?" Terence says.

"You've been through a very tough time," Dad says, "way tougher than most kids your age have to go through. You lost your mom, your school, most of your friends in the process."

"Yeah," Terence says, feeling a tear starting.

Dad takes Terence's hand on the table between them. "Here's what I think, and you can do whatever you want with this," Dad says.

Terence stares at their hands.

"Eddie sounds like a good friend," he says. "And she's a terrific singer too. Your band, from what I've heard, is fantastic and you're bound to do well and at least have a very good time at the battle tomorrow — if you choose to join in. I think you might regret it if you don't."

"But there's another thing," Dad goes on, "and in a way it might be more important. Your mom loved music. She loved *your* music, and if she could be here right now . . . ," Dad trails off, and Terence looks up to find his father shaking his head slowly, a sad smile on his face. "She'd be so proud of you, Terence. *She'd* want you to be up on that stage."

Dad squeezes Terence's hand and lets it go. He takes a drink of his pop, puts the cap on, and puts it back in the fridge. "Are you hungry?"

"Not really," Terence says, wiping his eyes.

Dad sniffs, his back to Terence, as he opens the cupboard. "Well, good. I haven't been to the grocery store since I started this new job. We're essentially out of food."

"I guess I better text Eddie," Terence says.

"That's a good idea," Dad says, "and I'll call Paulie's. You'll get hungry when the pizza shows up, I have a feeling."

Smiling now, Terence hurries to his room and dives onto his bed, grabbing his phone. He fires off a group text first:

Can everyone get together um right now for a last-minute rehearsal. Sorry btw.

And then another to Eddie:

Thanks.

Dad makes Terence eat pizza — "Because if you don't then I'll eat it and honestly I've been stress-eating enough, thank you" — before they get in the car and head to the Viateurs'.

Dad parks and switches off the car.

"Um, you're coming in?" Terence says with one foot out the door.

"Sure," Dad says. "Seems like about time I meet some of your friends' parents, right?"

"Right," Terence says, unsure. But he and Dad approach the front door together, and Ms. Viateur lets them in.

"I'm Raymond Kato," Dad says, smiling.

Ms. Viateur smiles. "So glad to meet you. It's been so nice having your son over so much these past few months. I love the kids' music."

The two adults smile down at Terence.

"The talent these kids have at such a young age . . . ," Ms. Viateur says, beaming.

"It really is something," Dad says, and he smiles and musses Terence's hair.

"All right," Terence says, moving farther into the house. "Is everyone down there already."

"Yup!" Ms. V says as she closes the door.

Terence hurries down the basement steps just as Ms. V says to his father, "Come in and sit for a while. Would you like some tea or something?"

"There he is!" Claude shouts from the piano, playing a fanfare.

Eddie, James, and Novia all smile up at him when he stops halfway down the steps.

"Oh good," Terence says. "Three phony smiles."

"I'm smiling too," Claude says from behind the piano.

"Four, then," Terence says, coming all the way down the steps.

Eddie meets him at the bottom with a hug. "I'm sorry too," she says. "And thank *you* too."

"Me?" Terence says back. "What'd I do?"

"You started this band," she says. "You got me singing. Out loud."

"Oh," Terence says. "Good."

Eddie nods and runs back to the couch. "Now let's do this. We have a set to rehearse."

"Can we just be clear about one thing first?" James says, raising his hand. "Are we or are we not playing the battle of the bands tomorrow?"

"We are," Terence says.

The other cheer.

"That's why we have a lot of work to do tonight," Terence says.

Novia leans on her harp. "I don't know," she says. "It's only three songs, right? One per round?"

"If we last all three rounds," James says.

"We will," Terence says, "and yes, it's just three songs, including we've never played. Well, most of us."

"Huh?" Claude says.

"You show up after two weeks gone," James says, "and just drop a new song on us? You crazy?"

"Crazy like a fox," Terence says. "I think it'll be worth it."

"So what song?" Novia asks. "Another jazz standard?"

"Zeppelin?" Claude says.

"Something current?" James says.

"Very current," Terence says, looking at Eddie. "It's not even out yet."

"What?" Eddie says. "What are you talking about, Weird Terry?"

Terence laughs. "It goes something like . . . ," he says, and then sings what he can remember of Eddie's song — the one she's been writing all spring and Terence overheard back in January and again in March.

Eddie covers her open mouth with her hand and blushes. Terence feels his face go hot too.

"What is that?" Claude says, trying to find the chords.

Novia picks at her strings, looking for right sound to match what Terence sang. "Sing it again," she says.

Terence shakes his head. "Eddie will sing," he says, and he reaches under the couch for the old acoustic. "She wrote it."

Eddie accepts the guitar and sits on the couch.

"You write songs?" James says.

"A little," Eddie admits. "I didn't know you heard me," she adds to Terence.

"Well, I did," he says, "and I'm sorry I didn't listen to you when you told me about your songs months ago."

She strums the opening chord slowly and quietly. "Are you sure about this?"

"Play it, Eddie!" Novia smiles.

"OK, OK," Eddie says. "Don't judge me too harshly." And she plays.

The PA Quintet practices the new song and the other two songs for the battle tomorrow until almost ten. Finally, when their rendition of "Now At Last" comes to an end, Ms. V pops her head in the door at the top of the basement steps. "I think it's time to wrap up now, guys!"

"OK, Mom!" Claude says. "Pack it up!"

While Terence puts his bass away, Eddie sits on the arm of the couch beside him. "Thanks," she says quietly.

"It's a great song," Terence says.

Eddie bites her fingernail. "You think so?"

Terence nods.

"You think people will like it tomorrow?" Eddie asks.

"Definitely," Terence says.

James, with his laptop in one hand, walks by them to head upstairs. "Relax," he says. "It's a good song." He goes upstairs.

Claude and Novia carry the harp up.

"Really good, Eddie," Novia says as they pass.

Claude winks.

"See?" Terence says.

Eddie smiles. "Well, I did try to tell you on the bus that morning," she says. "Should've listened."

"There's the Eddie I know," Terence says. "And you're right." He puts his gig bag on his shoulder and together they head upstairs.

"There you are," Terence's dad says when they reach the kitchen. To everyone's surprise, he and Ms. and Mr. Viateur have been joined by Ms. Carson and Novia's dad too.

"Uh-oh," Eddie says. "What have you old people been up to?"

"Just telling embarrassing stories," Ms. Carson says.

"Sharing baby photos," Terence's dad says.

"Stuff like that," Novia's dad says.

"See you all at the battle tomorrow?" Dad says, hopping down from his stool at the island.

The other parents agree they wouldn't miss it, and Terence and his dad head home.

In the car, Terence's eyes are heavy. He reclines the seat a little stares at the moon, which seems to follow their car as it cruises along the almost empty streets.

"Thanks, Dad," he says.

"Hm?" Dad says. "For what?"

"Driving."

CHAPTER FIVE

The battle begins at one the next day, and though he knows he should eat and though Claude shows up and immediately suggests the whole band has lunch together, Terence can hardly take a bite of his sandwich.

Across from him, Eddie isn't eating either. "I can't," she says. "My tummy is doing backflips right now."

Claude leans across the table. "I'll have yours," he says, snatching it up.

Eddie slaps his hand, but he manages to take a bite anyway before putting it back.

"Everyone knows the set list?" Terence says.

"Yes, Terence, yes," James says, rolling his eyes. "We know the *three-song* set list. It's not hard to remember a *three-song* set list."

"I just wanna be sure," Terence says, slumping in his seat.

From his seat, he can look out the doorway to the sandwich shop and watch the Saturday lunchtime crowds pass by. People of all shapes and sizes and colors walk by, leisurely passing the morning and afternoon at the mall, none as nervous as he is.

One of them, though, perhaps is: in a group of old friends, her auburn hair in a bun at the top of her head and dressed in a long black dress — like she's performing in a cabaret, rather than an atrium at the mall — is Polly Winger.

She's only there for an instant — as long as it takes for a group of fourteen-year-olds, excited

and nervous and full of energy — to walk by an
open doorway at the mall. But it's enough.

Terence leans forward. "Guys, two things."

Everyone stops chewing to look at Terence.

"One," he says, "we have to win. My band
from Hart is here, and they're in the battle."

"For sure," James says. "They're toast."

"What's the other thing?" Novia says before
slurping pop up a straw.

"Two," Terence continues, "I didn't know it
was possible, but I just got even more nervous."

Terence is kneeling on the floor of a
bathroom stall when someone thumps on the
stall door.

"You OK in there, T?" James says. "Need
me to . . . I don't know. Find your dad or
something?"

Terence shakes his head and wipes his
mouth. "I'm fine," he says. "Just a nervous . . .
nervous . . . stomach."

"OK," James says. "Might wanna come on out of there, though. It's like five to one."

"OK," Terence says. He watches James's feet disappear under the stall, counts to ten, checks for queasiness in his tummy, and leaves the stall. After washing his face and hands and gargling a few times, he hurries out of the bathroom.

"Finally," Eddie says. "Come *on*, guys."

Then the PA Quintet are hurrying through the mall, dodging around families and strollers and high schoolers and retirees, making their way to the atrium.

When they arrive, the stage is built, the crowd assembled, and a banner hangs over the back of the stage: *Fourteenth Annual Battle of the KID Bands.*

"Stupidest name ever," James says, shaking his head.

"Well, it's the last time you'll be able to enter," Eddie says, clapping his shoulder, "if it's any consolation."

"Oh yeah," James says, screwing up his eyebrows. "That kinda stinks."

The five stride to the side of the stage. "And this must be . . . ," says the man with the clipboard, "the Public Announcement Quintet."

"Just PA Quintet is fine too," Eddie pipes up.

"Got it," the man says, grinning at her. "Hey, I liked your demo."

"What?" James says. "You heard it?"

"My kid had it on her phone," he says.

"Does she go to Franklin Middle School?" Terence asks.

He shakes his head. "North End High," he says.

"I don't even know where that is," Eddie whispers to Novia. They both giggle, and Terence shushes them.

"Anyway, you're checked in," the clipboard man says. "In the first round, you guys are up — one, two, three . . . sixth. You're up sixth."

"Out of how many?" Claude asks.

"We have sixteen bands competing this year," clipboard man says. "Twice as many as last year. It's going to be a fun day."

"A long day too," James says.

"You can hang out in the 'green room,'" says clipboard man, putting air quotes around "green room." He nods toward a little curtained-off area behind the stage, where they can see some other kids and tables and chairs set up, along with bottles of pop and bags of chips.

Among them, Terence finds Polly Winger.

"Guys," he says, "I'll be right back."

"Is that her?" Eddie says, grabbing his arm and squinting into the green room. "The one in the cocktail dress?"

Terence nods.

"I already don't like her," Eddie says.

"Be right back," Terence says.

He walks into the green room. As soon as he steps foot inside, someone jumps up from Polly's table and holds up a hand to stop him.

"Sorry, kid," he says. "This area is for the talent only."

"Knock it off, Harrison," Terence says, for this is Harrison Engel, one-time guitar player in the Kato Quintet at Hart. "You know I'm here for the battle too."

Harrison squints at him. "Terence?" he says, as if a fog is lifting. "Terence Kato? Is that you? I — I didn't even recognize you. How long has it been? Oh, it's been too, too long. . . ."

"You're hilarious, Harrison," Terence says, dodging around the boy and stepping up to Polly's seat. "I wanted to say good luck." He puts out his hand.

Polly puts her hand in his, but not like a shake. More like a queen offering a peasant her ring to kiss. "*We*," she says, "won't need luck. *We* are virtuosos."

Terence looks down at her — though she won't look at him at all — and he fights the anger rising in his belly. "I'm sorry I didn't stay in touch," he says quietly. "It was . . . a tough winter."

She withdraws her hand and says, "I know."

"OK," Terence says. "Well, good luck."

She looks up at him finally, her eyes shaded under long lashes and loose curls across her forehead, and replies, "Good luck."

Terence returns to his bandmates just outside the green room.

"Let's watch the first five bands," Novia says. "It seems polite."

There are plenty of seats out front still. "Might help to fill the seats too," James says.

"The turnout is a little leaner than I thought it would be," Terence admits as they find an empty bench and sit down.

"Fine with me," Eddie says, rubbing her palms on her frayed jeans. "Makes me a little less nervous."

Just then, clipboard man — now without his clipboard — climbs the stage and walks to the mic. "Ladies and gentlemen, welcome to the fourteenth annual Wellstone Music Store's — on Old Main Street at the corner of 33rd Avenue — Battle of the Kid Bands!"

The crowd claps. A few people — including Claude — hoot and holler. Passersby slow down or stop. A few even take a seat.

"We've got a whole slew of bands coming up, so let me run down quickly how this works," clipboard man says. "First round — which will begin in a few seconds — we'll hear one song from each of the sixteen bands in today's battle. The judges will eliminate *half* of those bands, and they *will* consider audience reaction.

"In round two," clipboard continues, "we'll hear a different song from the surviving eight bands. Then we'll be left with our three finalists, who will each perform a third song beginning at six this evening."

The five members of the PAQ all look at each other, hearts in their throats.

"So without further ado," says clipboard man, "let's bring out our first band, from way out in River Bluff, the Screaming Pachyderms!"

The fifth band — Red Yellow and Blue, from River City — is just about finished when Terence leads the PAQ to the stage.

"You ready?" says clipboard man over the chaotic noise of the Red Yellow and Blue, who have been thrashing around on stage, banging garbage can lids together and screaming at each other in what must be Martian.

"We're ready," Terence says.

"As soon as this . . . band," clipboard man shouts over the din, "finishes this . . . song, be ready to load in, all right?"

"Load in?" Eddie shouts back.

"Put your stuff on the stage and plug in," clipboard man explains.

He heads off to attend to clipboard-man business.

"Are we ready?" Terence says to his friends in a huddle behind the stage.

Novia nods and pats her harp case.

Claude cracks his knuckles. "Let's do this."

"Yeah, yeah," James says. "Pep talk, pep talk, blah blah. They're done. Let's get up there!"

"Um, hi," Eddie says into the mic to the smattering of a crowd at their feet. The speakers squeak in protest, and she backs off the mic a bit. "We're the PA Quintet, from Franklin Middle School, right here in town."

"And East High!" James says, leaning into her mic.

Eddie shoves him back to his gear. "Anyway, this one is a classic by Gerald Marks and Seymour Simons, from way back in 1931."

A few people in the audience whisper.

"We've brought it out of the Stone Age," Eddie adds, smiling, and Claude plays the intro to "All of Me."

They play it slow and sparse. Eddie's vocals are powerful and rich, but slow and under control. James's beats suit her singing style, keeping everything laid back and cool, while Novia's hard playing gives the whole piece an eerie and almost mysterious air.

Terence couldn't be happier, and though he couldn't see Eddie's face from his position behind her, he could tell she was pleased too.

"That was amazing!" Eddie says as they climb down from the stage after the song.

"It was," Terence says, letting her throw her arms around his neck. "You were great."

"Hey, where's my hug?" Claude says. "I was great too."

The big eighth-grader throws his arms around Terence, and soon all five of the PA Quintet are in a group hug behind the stage.

"I have to admit," says Polly as she and her band make their way to take the stage. "That was good. You'll survive the round for sure."

"Don't sound so surprised," Eddie says, glaring at her.

Polly shrugs one shoulder. "I'm not," she says. "Honest." She flashes a big smile, climbs the steps to the stage, and steps up to the microphone.

"We're the Winger Five," she says, "from Hart Arts Academy here in River City. This one's called 'I'm Gonna Sit Right Down and Write Myself a Letter.'"

It's one that Terence taught her a year and a half ago. She'd never even heard of the Great American Songbook back then.

"Now look at her," Terence mumbles.

"Do I have to?" Eddie says. She shrugs. "She's good."

"She is," Terence says.

"All right, all right," Eddie says. "She's great." She listens for a bit. "Do you have this song?"

"Of course," Terence says. "Actually, I have a recording of Polly singing it too."

Eddie sneers, but then says, "Send it to me?"

Terence laughs. "You got it."

The PA Quintet survive the first round, as do the Winger Five. The second round begins at four, and this time the PAQ is up first.

Their rendition of "Now At Last" is cool and crisp, and while he's playing, Terence forgets it's warm outside today, even for spring.

The song and Eddie's voice are like a blanket of snow on a gray morning, James's beats and Novia's harp like the sun breaking through and reflecting off the snow, and Claude's piano playing like the cracking puddles underfoot. Terence hopes his bass is like the earth it all lies on top of.

The crowd is larger now, though Terence hardly notices until the song is finished and the crowd cheers.

The Winger Five play last in the second round. Polly steps up to the mic.

"Before we start," she says, "I just want to say thanks and good luck to all the other bands playing today — especially to the PA Quintet."

"What?" James says.

"If it weren't for Terence Kato," Polly goes on, "the Winger Five wouldn't even exist."

The audience slowly comes around and claps halfheartedly at Polly's urging.

"Now we're going to play 'Here Comes the Sun,'" Polly says, and she turns to the band to count them in.

"What was that about?" Eddie asks Terence.

He can only shrug.

"Must be trying to throw you off," James says, leaning across Eddie to whisper to Terence. "Confuse you. She knows we'll be in the finals."

"Maybe," Terence says. It doesn't sound like something Polly would do, but maybe she's changed a lot since they used to hang out.

Polly bows after their rendition of the Beatles song, and she and her band leave the stage.

Clipboard man comes on clapping. "Weren't they great?" he says when he reaches the mic. "That was the Winger Five, and the last of our semifinalists this afternoon."

Clipboard man claps, and the crowd follows his lead with another round of applause.

"We're going to take five now," clipboard man goes on, "and I'll be back with the judges' choices for our three finalists. Sit tight."

"What do you guys think?" Terence asks when he and the rest of the PAQ have claimed a table in the shrinking green room.

"We're in," James says. "No doubt."

"I don't know," Novia says, drumming her long, skilled fingers on the green paper tablecloth. "Polly's band is really good, and those two bands from Upper Prince River were good too."

"That makes three," Eddie says.

"We were better than all of them," Claude insists, high-fiving James.

"Maybe," Terence says. "But Polly's band and us, we're both jazz. Or mostly jazz. What if they want a bigger variety?"

James crosses his arms. "We're not jazz."

Eddie cocks her head. "Um, we are though?"

James shakes his head. "We're trip-hop."

"Maybe," Terence says. "Not sure it's enough. The bands from Upper Prince are hard rock and country. It's like a lineup made for a final round: the perfect variety of American music."

The other fall silent and sit like that for a minute. Their anxious reverie is interrupted by clipboard man.

"All right, everyone," he says to the eight remaining acts, patting his clipboard. "I'm about to make the announcement. We've got the front rows set aside for you all."

"Good luck, Terence," Polly Winger says as she leads her band to the benches.

"You too," Terence says back, smiling.

"She's trying to throw you off," James hisses at him, but Terence ignores him.

When everyone is seated, clipboard man walks up to the mic. "I have here," he says, again patting his clipboard, "the names of the three acts that will perform right here in the finals tonight."

The crowd — made up of the eight surviving bands and their friends and families — cheers.

"First," clipboard man says, "from Upper Prince River, the Glass Banana!"

The hard rock four-piece jumps to their feet and high-five each other, and then run up on stage.

"And our second finalist," clipboard man goes on as the applause dies down, "from right here in River City . . ."

Terence leans forward and pumps his fists.

Clipboard man finishes, "The Winger Five!"

Terence sags, and quickly sits up straight and claps as Polly and her band walk onto the stage.

"And our last finalist today," clipboard man says.

Eddie grabs Terence's hand and squeezes it tight.

Clipboard continues, "Also from right here in River City . . ."

Terence is almost on his feet.

"The PA Quintet!"

Terence and his friends practically jump onto the stage, arms around each other in celebration.

He glances at Polly, who smiles at him across the stage and waves.

"In an hour," he says to Eddie, "one of us could be the champs of the battle."

Eddie looks across the stage at Terence's former bandmates. "And the other . . ."

"Won't be."

CHAPTER SIX

The PAQ are gathered at the bottom of the stage steps, ready to load-in.

"Guys," Eddie says, "it's not too late for us to play 'Shine a Light On' instead."

"Don't be ridiculous," Novia says. "We haven't played that in weeks."

"Besides," Terence says, "your song is going to kill."

Eddie takes a deep, fast breath between clenched teeth and looks up at the stage.

The Glass Banana is nearly finished with their third-round song — a 21 Pilots cover. It's good. If the judges are looking for a more marketable sound, these guys have it in the bag.

They finish up, bow quickly, and come down the steps past the PAQ.

"Good luck, you guys," the lead singer says.

"Thanks," Novia says. "You guys sounded great."

Eddie turns to Terence and takes him by both shoulders. "I need you to give me some confidence," she says, lowering her gaze.

Terence thinks for a minute, while onstage the clipboard man begins their introduction.

"Our next finalist," he announces, "is the Public Announcement Quintet, of River City."

"When I was new at Franklin Middle School," Terence says quickly, looking into Eddie's eyes, "you were the only person I wanted to see each day."

"Yeah?" she says.

"They got their first taste of local fame," the clipboard man goes on, "when their demo songs were played over the PA system at East High."

Terence nods. "And when I heard your voice in the school basement that first day," he goes on, "I knew we were meant to play together and do something amazing."

"Please put your hands together," clipboard man says, "for the band PA Quintet!"

Eddie's nervous frown bends into a smile as the other band members head onstage to quickly set up.

"And we have," Terence finishes.

"OK," Eddie says, pulling him against her for a hug. "Let's do this."

Hand in hand, they take the stage.

"I'm a little nervous about this," Eddie says into the mic, and the audience smiles and laughs and claps. "Our next song is . . . well, I wrote it."

The crowd is the biggest it's been all day, with Terence's dad, the Carsons, the Viateurs, the Paganos, and even James's parents in the front row. When *they* cheer, it spreads backward through the crowd until everyone is clapping and hooting — even Polly's Winger Five.

"Thank you," Eddie says, glancing at Terence. "It's called 'Within, Without.'"

She lowers her head as Novia starts the song. At the fourth bar, the rest of the band joins in, and then Eddie begins to sing at the next bar.

Terence has heard the song before, obviously, but this evening he closes his eyes and lets his fingers move on their own, and he listens. It's a song about what's inside her, and what she shows the world. In a way, though, it's a song about what's inside everyone.

Eddie holds the last note — a C at the top of her range — as long as she ever has, and before she ends the song, the crowd is on their feet.

She bows, and she motions to the rest of the band. Terence bows too, and Claude gets up from his keyboard. Even James is smiling as he steps from behind the table he's got his laptop set up on to bow. Novia manages to awkwardly rise under the weight of the harp too, before Claude hurries over to help her stand.

The PAQ join hands and bow together, and then hurry from the stage.

"What is taking so long?" Eddie says, pacing in front of the stage.

"You have to relax," Claude says. "Have something to eat."

Eddie shakes her head. "I can't eat," she says.

Terence can hardly keep his seat too, and hasn't touched the Chinese takeout his father bought for the band after the third round.

"I don't know what you're so nervous about," James says, shoveling vegetable lo mein into his face.

"Yeah," Novia says. "Glass Banana probably won anyway."

"No!" Eddie says. "Don't say that!"

Novia shrugs. "Easier to expect the worse," she says. "Then if it doesn't happen, great! If it does, at least you were ready."

Terence watches clipboard man, who is sitting at a table with the judges: the owner of Wellstone Music Store, the talent booker at a famous downtown club, and a local blogger. They're in a heated debate, and Terence would love to go over and eavesdrop.

Soon, though, clipboard rises from the table and walks over to them. "Kids," he says, gathering the PAQ, the Winger Five, and the Glass Banana into a semicircle around him. "I'll be announcing the winner in ten minutes."

The PA Quintet sit together on one bench, huddling close as if they're watching the same horror movie.

Eddie takes Terence's hand. "I can't take it."

"I'm nervous too," Terence says, "but if we don't win, I think I'll be OK."

"Why?" Eddie says.

"Because I'm living my life," Terence says, smiling at her, "and I've got some great friends to do that with."

Eddie's expression softens as color rises in her cheeks.

Clipboard man finally takes the stage and steps up to the mic. "Before I announce this year's winner," he says, "I have to take a few minutes to thank all our sponsors."

A groan rises from the crowd, but he goes on undeterred, listing the names of a dozen local businesses who supported the battle.

"And finally," he says, "to announce this year's winner. We had a great battle — the largest we've ever had, and every act who played today deserves a round of applause."

Everyone claps.

"I hope they'll all keep playing music," clipboard man says. "Today's first-place winner — the winner of recording studio time, a spot on the local bands compilation we produce each year with radio station SEBB-FM, and ten *thousand* dollars — is . . ."

They all lean forward on the bench.

"Glass Banana!"

The four members of Glass Banana, arm in arm, hurry onstage to accept their award.

Terence is about ready to just get up and walk away, when clipboard man steps up to the mic again. "This year we have a special award, as well," he announces to settle down the crowd.

"Now, it took some special conniving at the judges' table," he goes on with a chuckle, "but we came up with a great solution — and a special award for this year's best original song."

Eddie sits up.

Terence puts a hand on her arm. "Wait a second," he says. "Is he serious?"

Eddie's eyes go wide.

"Receiving a prize of recording studio time and a spot on our compilation," clipboard man says, "is the Public Announcement Quintet for their original song by Meredith Carson, 'Within, Without'! Come on up, PAQ!"

Together, the five bandmates run onstage to accept their impromptu award.

Terence looks out at the crowd and finds his father, standing on a bench at the back so he can see over everyone's heads. He's grinning and clapping and shouting out Terence's name.

The five members of the PAQ join hands again to bow, and Terence realizes how happy he is. He's onstage with his four best friends, a group he never would have believed if he weren't a part of it.

For an instant, his heart hurts, because he's happy even though his mother is gone. But the instant passes quickly, and he reminds himself that this is the life his mother wanted for him: one filled with friends and music and joy.

And remembering her well means living it every day.

MUSIC TRIVIA

Think you have what it takes to join Terence Kato's band? Take this music trivia quiz and find out!

1. What is the level and intensity of sound measured in?
   A. Decibels
   B. Gigabytes
   C. Vibrato

2. A musical scale comprises how many notes?
   A. 16
   B. 8
   C. 10

3. What term describes people singing without instruments?
   A. Solo
   B. Allegro
   C. A cappella

4. What term describes the section of a song that is repeated after each verse?
   A. Beat
   B. Chorus
   C. Choir

5. What term describes how high or low a musical sound is?
   A. Pitch
   B. Range
   C. Volume

6. What is the highest singing voice called?
   A. Baritone
   B. Tenor
   C. Soprano

7. How many musical instruments make up a quartet?
   A. 4
   B. 14
   C. 8

8. What Italian word means "growing louder?"
   A. Crescendo
   B. Bass
   C. Allegro

9. What are all instruments that are played by being hit with something called?
   A. Brass
   B. Woodwinds
   C. Percussion

10. What is the lowest singing voice called?
    A. Baritone
    B. Tenor
    C. Soprano

Answers: 1. A 2. B 3. C 4. B 5. A 6. C
7. A 8. A 9. C 10. A

STEVE BREZENOFF

Steve Brezenoff is the author of more than fifty middle-grade chapter books, including the Field Trip Mysteries series, the Ravens Pass series of thrillers, and the Return to the Titanic series. He's also written three young-adult novels, *Guy in Real Life*; *Brooklyn, Burning*; and *The Absolute Value of -1*. In his spare time, he enjoys video games, cycling, and cooking. Steve lives in Minneapolis with his wife, Beth, and their son and daughter.